P9-DDU-542

# THE SINGING CHICK

**VICTORIA STENMARK** · ILLUSTRATED BY **RANDY CECIL**

HENRY HOLT AND COMPANY · NEW YORK

Henry Holt and Company, Inc., *Publishers since 1866*
115 West 18th Street, New York, New York 10011

Henry Holt is a registered trademark of Henry Holt and Company, Inc.
Text copyright © 1999 by Igor Stenmark. Illustrations copyright © 1999 by Randy Cecil
Published in Canada by Fitzhenry & Whiteside Ltd., 195 Allstate Parkway, Markham, Ontario L3R 4T8.

Library of Congress Cataloging-in-Publication Data
Stenmark, Victoria. The singing chick / Victoria Stenmark; illustrated by Randy Cecil.
Summary: A newly hatched, happily singing chick is eaten by a fox, who then starts singing before being
eaten by a wolf, and so begins a chain of eating and singing for a series of animals. [1. Animals—Fiction.
2. Singing—Fiction.] I. Cecil, Randy, ill. II. Title. PZ7.S8289Si 1999 [E]—dc21 98-6609

ISBN 0-8050-5255-0  First Edition—1999
The artist used oil paint on paper to create the illustrations for this book.
Printed in the United States of America on acid-free paper. ∞
1 3 5 7 9 10 8 6 4 2

For Daniel
—V. S.

For my nephew Cayden
—R. C.

On a warm, sunny day in the middle of the forest, a white egg was lying on the ground.

CRACK!!!

The egg broke in two, and out jumped a fluffy yellow chick. The chick looked around.
"How beautiful everything is!" he exclaimed. And off he went, skipping through the forest and singing a song he had just made up.

"The sky is so blue!
The sun is so yellow!

The trees are so green!
And I'm a happy fellow!

*Peep-peep! Peep-peep! Pirrippi! Peep-peep-peep!"*

The singing chick had barely finished the last line of his song when he saw a fox walking out of the bushes.

"Hello, Fox," said the chick.

"Hello, Lunch," said the fox, licking his lips. And he swallowed the singing chick in one big gulp.

The fox patted his full stomach, but suddenly he felt funny.

*"The sky is so blue!"* he sang.
Why did I say that? he wondered.
*"The sun is so yellow!"* he sang
again, louder this time.

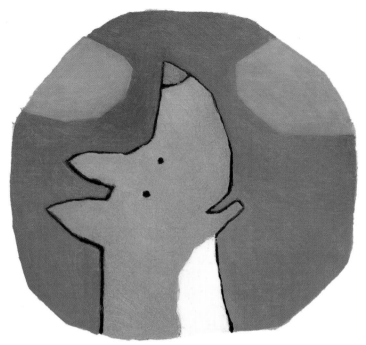

He clasped his paws over
his mouth, but it didn't help.
*"The trees are so green! And
I'm a happy fellow!"* he sang
as loudly as he could.

And off he went skipping through the forest,
yelling, *"Peep-peep! Peep-peep! Pirrippi! Peep-peep-peep!"*

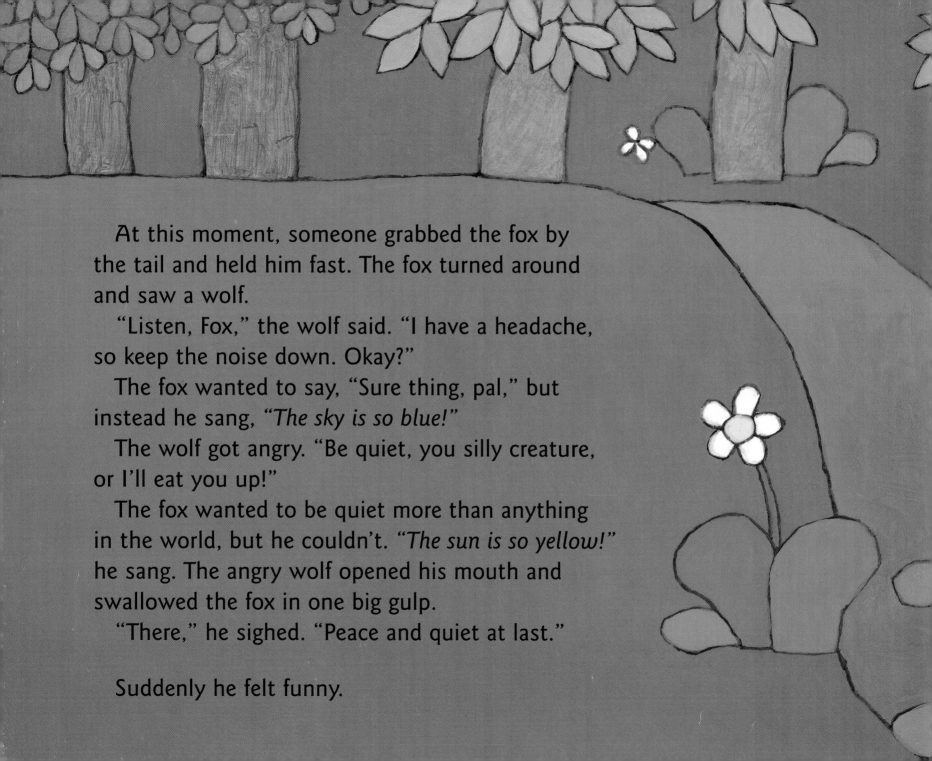

At this moment, someone grabbed the fox by the tail and held him fast. The fox turned around and saw a wolf.

"Listen, Fox," the wolf said. "I have a headache, so keep the noise down. Okay?"

The fox wanted to say, "Sure thing, pal," but instead he sang, *"The sky is so blue!"*

The wolf got angry. "Be quiet, you silly creature, or I'll eat you up!"

The fox wanted to be quiet more than anything in the world, but he couldn't. *"The sun is so yellow!"* he sang. The angry wolf opened his mouth and swallowed the fox in one big gulp.

"There," he sighed. "Peace and quiet at last."

Suddenly he felt funny.

*"The trees are so green! And I'm a happy fellow!"* he sang.

"Oh-oh," said the wolf. "I'm afraid that fox didn't agree with me."

His legs started skipping up and down all by themselves. And off he went, wailing at the top of his lungs, *"Peep-peep! Peep-peep! Pirrippi . . ."*

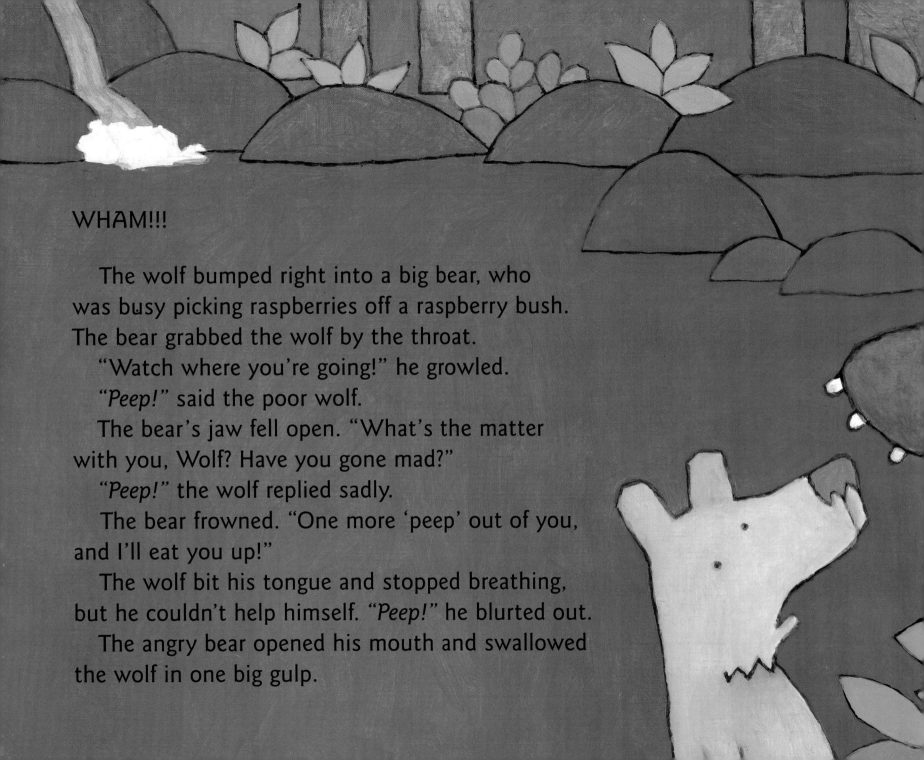

WHAM!!!

The wolf bumped right into a big bear, who was busy picking raspberries off a raspberry bush. The bear grabbed the wolf by the throat.

"Watch where you're going!" he growled.

"*Peep!*" said the poor wolf.

The bear's jaw fell open. "What's the matter with you, Wolf? Have you gone mad?"

"*Peep!*" the wolf replied sadly.

The bear frowned. "One more 'peep' out of you, and I'll eat you up!"

The wolf bit his tongue and stopped breathing, but he couldn't help himself. "*Peep!*" he blurted out.

The angry bear opened his mouth and swallowed the wolf in one big gulp.

Immediately he felt funny.

He started skipping, murmuring the song under his breath. Finally, off he went, scared out of his wits, growling,

*"The sky is so blue!*
*The sun is so yellow!*
*(What's happening to me?)*
*And I'm a happy fellow!*

*Peep-peep! (HELP!!!) Peep-peep!"*

The bear skipped through the thicket until he came to a high hill, and went on skipping up the hill to the top.

Suddenly he stumbled and
rolled back down toward a big
tree standing at the bottom.

BOOM!!!

The bear crashed into the tree.

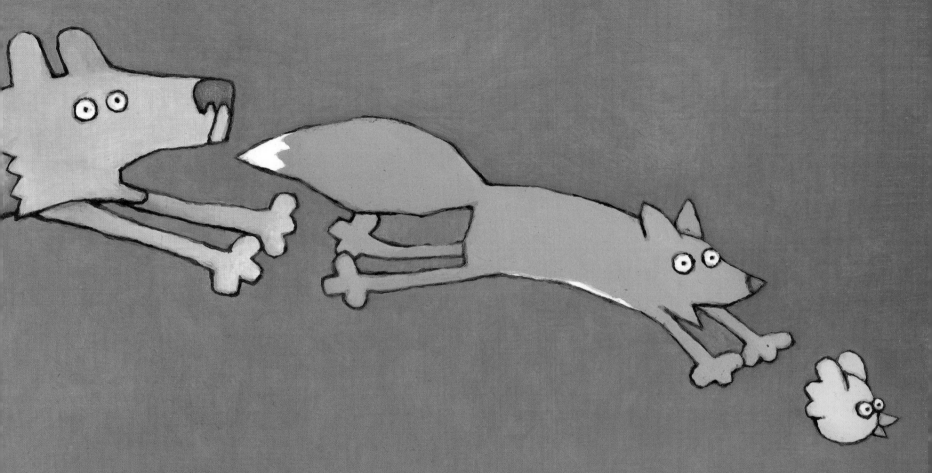

The wolf popped out of the bear's mouth.

The fox popped out of the wolf's mouth.

The singing chick popped out of the fox's mouth.

AND THEY ALL
STOPPED SINGING!

The bear, the wolf, and the fox were so happy,
they hugged and kissed the singing chick.

Then they took him
to the neighboring village,

to the henhouse, where he found his father—

and his mother, the singing hen.

And they all lived happily ever after.